# Lettice

## The Fairy Ball

For Anne Elizabeth Mary Brown (Mum)
with lots of love and fairy kisses,
Manny

A special thank you to Alison Sage

First published in hardback in Great Britain by HarperCollins Children's Books in 2006
First published in paperback in 2007
This edition published in 2010

1 3 5 7 9 10 8 6 4 2

ISBN: 978-0-00-782683-4

HarperCollins Children's Books is a division of HarperCollins Publishers Ltd.

Text and illustrations copyright © Mandy Stanley 2006

Visit our website at: www.harpercollins.co.uk

Printed in China

# Lettice

## The Fairy Ball

### Mandy Stanley

HarperCollins *Children's Books*

Lettice Rabbit and her family lived high up on top of a hill. Nibble, nibble, hop, hop, every day was the same, until one summer afternoon...

Lettice was making daisy chains
when she felt a sharp tug...

The daisy chain
s-t-r-e-t-c-h-e-d and,
*ping*, it broke and
whisked away.

Two tiny figures with
shimmering wings were
pulling it through the air.
'Stop!' shrieked Lettice.

All of a sudden, they
swooped down a hole in the
roots of an old oak.

Lettice pressed her nose
inside but she was too big to go
through. 'Who *are* you?' she cried.
'What are you *doing*?'

Lettice jumped back. Suddenly, in front of her, was a group of tiny people. 'Rabbit,' laughed one, 'our Queen needs your daisy chain for the Fairy Ball in Fairyland.'

'Fairyland?' squeaked Lettice.
'I'd like to go to Fairyland.
But I'm too big!'

'If you give us your chain, we will sprinkle fairy dust on you,' giggled a chorus of little voices, and the air filled with golden sparkles.

'Atishoo!'
sneezed Lettice.
Suddenly, she was
shrinking...

and shrinking...

and then she was
no bigger than an oak leaf!

Happily, Lettice
dashed into the hole
after the fairies.

Inside, it was dark, but soon
she came to a door and
through it was...

# FAIRYLAND!

'Quickly, now,' said the fairies, 'it's time to put on our best clothes to welcome the Queen.'

Lettice's face fell.
What was she going
to wear?

'Don't worry,' laughed
the fairies. 'Just
close your eyes!'
Lettice stood still.

She could feel
something soft and
light, smelling of
flowers, dropping
over her ears.

It was the prettiest
little fairy dress,
trimmed with
thistledown.

Just then, a bossy elf cried,
'Make way for Her Majesty, Queen Titania!'
The Fairy Queen had arrived!

She was riding in a carriage made of yellow rose
petals, drawn by a yellow bird, and her reins
were... Lettice's daisy chain!

'Welcome, little rabbit. Thank you for my beautiful reins,' smiled the Queen, holding out a tiny bracelet. 'This is for you. It will grant you one wish – use it well.'

Then young elves brought out the most wonderful fairy feast.

Afterwards, everyone danced
– especially Lettice!

All too soon it was time to go.
'We won't forget you, Lettice,'
called the fairies, waving goodbye.
'Wait!' squeaked Lettice. 'I'm still small!'

Just then, a cloud
of fairy dust floated
down, making Lettice's
nose twitch.

The ground felt all
wobbly and she was
growing bigger...

and bigger...

and bigger, until
she was the right size.

In two hops and a jump, Lettice was home. She bounced in to tell her family all about the fairies.

'They're ever so small and pretty,' she sighed.
'Oh, I *wish* you could see them, too.'

Just then, the magic bracelet on her paw glowed
and Lettice was sure she heard fairy laughter.

Lettice's brothers and sisters couldn't believe
their eyes! Fluttering above them were
hundreds of smiling fairies.

As she gazed up, Lettice murmured happily,
'My wish came true! I'm such a lucky rabbit.'

# Lettice

More dreams come true for
Lettice Rabbit in these
adorable picture books!

Lettice – The Dancing Rabbit
PB: 978-0-00-664777-5

Lettice – A Christmas Wish
PB: 978-0-00-716585-8

Lettice – The Bridesmaid
PB: 978-0-00-718407-1